**For Tim and Jackson
You're the best!**

Special thanks to all of our amazing friends and family who helped us get here.
You know who you are. We love you!

Written by Jan Helson & Rachel Annette Helson
Illustrated by Rachel Annette Helson
Cover Design & Interior Colors by David Brunell-Brutman

Printed in Canada by Friesens Corporation, Altona, MB, Canada, May 2012. Job # 74656
ISBN: 978-1-938511-00-4

A Pixel Entertainment Publication – www.pixelentertainment.com

Jan Helson & Rachel Annette Helson

THE GLOBAL GAME CHANGERS

The place is here. The time is now.

A figure zooms across the sky.
Is it a bird? Is it a plane?

No, it's a boy!

His name is **Little Big-Heart**,
and he is a superhero.

Little Big-Heart gets an alert from **Global Girl**, the leader of **The Global Game Changers**.

Global Girl

LBH, come to 🌍🏠 ASAP!

He rushes off to GGC Headquarters where Global Girl and her trusty dog, **Pixel**, are waiting for him.

"Little Big-Heart," exclaims Global Girl, "that dark cloud, **Krumi**, is spreading apathy, a disease where people don't care about each other. We need to recruit girls and boys throughout the world to help us fight!"

"Fight? Does that mean I have to use a weapon?" asks Little Big-Heart.

"*No!* The GGC don't fight people!" cries Global Girl. "We fight *for* people. We use our heads, hearts and hands to battle things like need, hunger and hurt."

"I know just where to start!" exclaims Little Big-Heart.
"If we build a strong alliance, we can destroy Krumi."

And in a flash, he races off to California.

He's looking for **Phoebe**, a little girl who collects food and delivers it to the San Francisco Food Bank. Krumi can't infect her because she is passionate about feeding hungry people.

He finds her!

"Phoebe," says Little Big-Heart, "You are a superhero!"

"But aren't superheroes grown-up people with magical powers?" she asks.

"No, a superhero is anyone who helps other people and doesn't expect anything in return," says Little Big-Heart. "We ignite good all over the world! Will you help us?"

"Absolutely,"
says Phoebe.

Little Big-Heart gives her a cape and a mobile device with a secret password to connect with the team back at Headquarters.

"Watch out for Krumi. He sneaks up on people very slowly."

"Oh! Don't worry!" says Phoebe as she waves good-bye to Little Big-Heart. "I'll be on the lookout."

"GGC *unite*!" Little Big-Heart cheers as he zooms away to Florida to find a boy named **Jaylen**.

JAYY-LEN!?

He lands at Jaylen's school.

But as he looks around for his next recruit, a giant hand picks Little Big-Heart up by the cape. It belongs to a big, mean bully.

UH-OH!

"Why are you wearing a cape with a weird symbol?" says the bully with a smirk.

Jaylen to the rescue!

"Stop being mean to him, you bully," Jaylen demands. The bully drops Little Big-Heart to the ground and stomps away.

"Bullies can be mean," Jaylen says as he helps Little Big-Heart get up. "I have something called Tourette's. It sometimes makes me say funny things and move around in unusual ways, so kids make fun of me a lot."

Out of the corner of his eye, Little Big-Heart spies Krumi snickering because everyone on the playground, except Jaylen, ignores the mean things that the bully does.

"They must hurt your feelings," says Little Big-Heart.

"They used to," Jaylen replies.

"But, one day I realized no one can make me feel bad about myself because I'm great just the way I am!"

"I started a group called Jaylen's Challenge to help stop bullying."

Jaylen notices the symbol on Little Big-Heart's cape.

"Hey," he exclaims, "you're part of the Global Game Changers! Can I join too? I want to fight Krumi by helping to ignite good in the world!"

"That's why I came! We really need you," says Little Big-Heart as he hands Jaylen his GGC gear.

"Just type in your password, and Global Girl will be waiting to video chat with you."

Little Big-Heart zooms off into the clouds.

Before he can get very far, he spots a woman sitting outside in the cold without any socks on her feet.

He sees people dressed warmly who walk by and don't even notice her.

Little Big-Heart spots Krumi, who is slowly spreading apathy all around them.

He tries to zap him with anti-apathy nanoparticles, but he misses, and Krumi gets away.

He stops and asks the woman, "Aren't your feet cold?"

"They are, but I don't have any money to pay for socks," she says.

"I know an awesome girl named **Hannah** who can help," says Little Big-Heart. "She started a group that collects socks and gives them to people who don't have any!"

They fly off to find Hannah together. *Whoosh!*

"There she is!" he exclaims.

"Hannah," says Little Big-Heart, "I've come because…."

But before he can finish his sentence, Hannah asks, "You're Little Big-Heart, aren't you?"

"I am," he says. "Can you help this woman get socks for her cold feet?"

"Of course," Hannah says as she hands the woman a pair of socks.

"Thank you," says the woman.

"Hannah," Little Big-Heart says, "you are a superhero because you help people in need. But two heads are always better than one. Will you join The Global Game Changers so we can work together to ignite good throughout the world?"

"I don't know," protests Hannah. "I'm only six. Won't the others be bigger than me?"

Little Big-Heart shows her the map on his GGC mobile device.

"All of the blinking red dots are six-year-old superheroes."

"See! Being little doesn't mean that you can't do BIG things!"

"*Wow*! I'm in!" Hannah exclaims.

Krumi is looming in the distance. He is *not* happy! The GGC Alliance is getting stronger everyday. They are igniting good everywhere so it is harder for Krumi to convince people not to care.

And at that moment, Little Big-Heart disappears. All of the Global Game Changers get a message on their mobile devices from Global Girl!

"Welcome new recruits! It's time to get started. Together we will work to defeat Krumi and ignite good. GGC *unite*!"

But, wait, where did Little Big-Heart
go? Is that him in the distance?

I think he's coming for...

You can be a Global Game Changer TOO!

Visit The Global Game Changers Headquarters at www.theglobalgamechangers.com, and join by sharing your Ignite Good story. You can cast your vote for which Global Game Changers charity you want to help, learn about other Global Game Changers just like you, and much more. Your actions count, and charities need your votes! Learn more about how you can make a difference, just like real-life Phoebe, Jaylen, and Hannah.